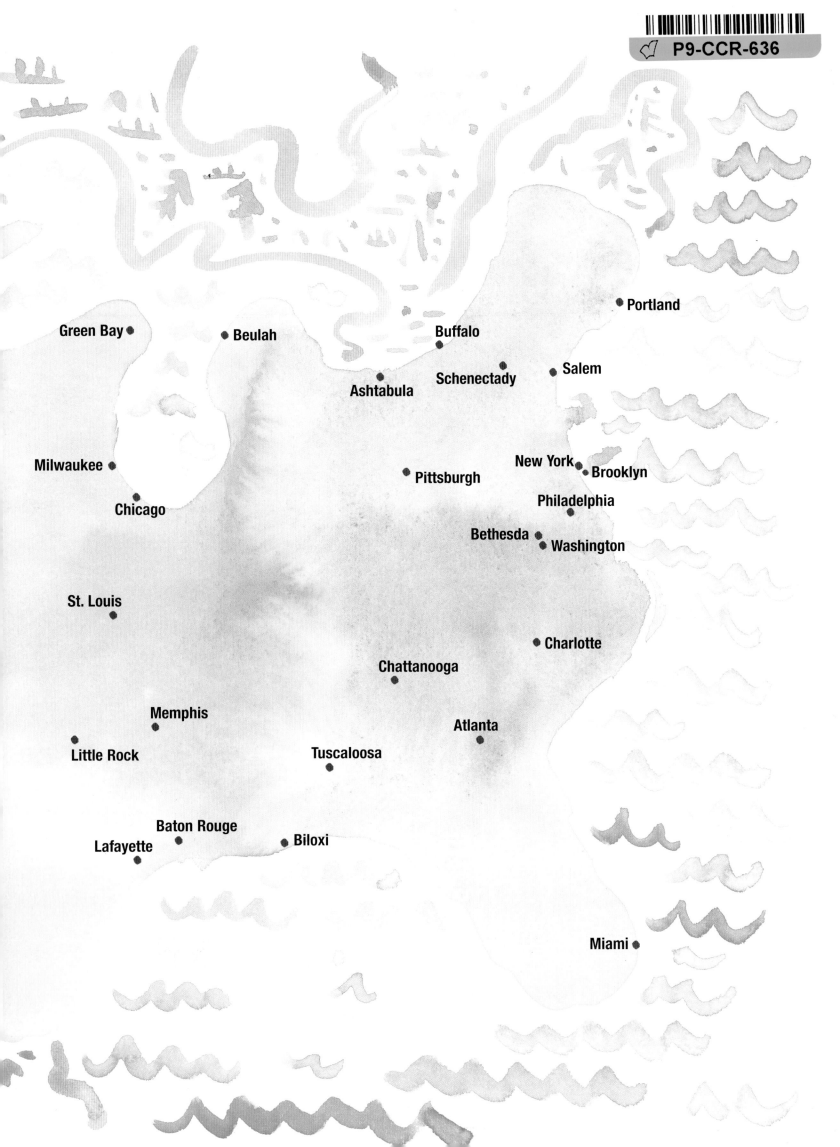

NEW YORK is English, CHATTANOOGA is Creek.

by chris raschka

A RICHARD JACKSON BOOK • Atheneum Books for Young Readers • New York   London   Toronto   Sydney

For Richard Jackson

Atheneum Books for Young Readers
An imprint of Simon & Schuster
Children's Publishing Division
1230 Avenue of the Americas, New York, New York 10020
Copyright © 2005 by Chris Raschka
Book design by Ann Bobco
The text for this book is set in
Golden Cockerel and HelveticaNeue Bold.
The illustrations for this book are
rendered in ink and watercolor.
Manufactured in China
First Edition
1 2 3 4 5 6 7 8 9 10
Library of Congress Cataloging-in-Publication Data
Raschka, Christopher.
New York is English, Chattanooga is Creek. /
Chris Raschka.—1st ed.
p. cm.
"A Richard Jackson Book."
Summary: New York City, though a bit boastful,
decides to throw a party to make new friends
of the other unique cities
like Chattanooga and Minneapolis.
ISBN 0-689-84600-2 (ISBN-13: 978-0-689-84600-7)
[1. Cities and towns—Fiction. 2. Names, Geographical—
Fiction. 3. Individuality—Fiction. 4. Parties—Fiction.]
I. Title.
PZ7.R1814Ne 2005
[E]—dc22 2004023188

GUEST LIST

Amarillo in Spanish means yellow. Yellow dirt nearby? Maybe. *(Amarillo, TX)*

Anchorage is English, and means a good place to tie up your boat. *(Anchorage, AK)*

Ashtabula in Algonquian means there are always enough moving. Perhaps they meant fish. *(Ashtabula, OH)*

Atlanta was made up in 1845 by J. E. Thomson to be the last stop on his Western and Atlantic Railroad Line. *(Atlanta, GA)*

Baton Rouge is French for red stick, one of which stood here as a hunting-ground boundary marker. *(Baton Rouge, LA)*

Bethesda is named in the Bible as a place where a pool of water was stirred by an angel. *(Bethesda, MD)*

Beulah is another Aramaic city name mentioned in the Bible. *(Beulah, MI)*

Brooklyn comes from the Dutch, *Breukelyn,* and might mean broken land. *(Brooklyn, NY)*

Buffalo could be French. *Beau fleuve* means beautiful river. *(Buffalo, NY)*

Charlotte is a German name. Charlotte Sophia married King George the Third in 1761. *(Charlotte, NC)*

Chattanooga is Creek for rocks rising to a point. It probably refers to Lookout Mountain. *(Chattanooga, TN)*

Cheyenne comes from the Dakota, *shia,* and means talkers. *(Cheyenne, WY)*

Chicago in Algonquian means stinking onions or onion place. Lots of wild onions and garlic grew where Chicago now stands. *(Chicago, IL)*

Des Moines is French for of the monks. However, the name might first have been des Moings, referring to a Native American community. *(Des Moines, IA)*

El Paso in Spanish means river crossing or passage. In 1598 Juan de Onate, traveling north, crossed the Rio Grande here. *(El Paso, TX)*

Green Bay is English, and means what it says. Maybe the water was greenish in the bay. *(Green Bay, WI)*

Lafayette is named for a French soldier, Marquis de Lafayette, a friend of George Washington, who came to fight for us in the Revolutionary War. *(Lafayette, LA)*

Las Vegas in Spanish means the meadows. It was probably a camping place. *(Las Vegas, NV)*

Little Rock is English. Apparently there was a bigger rock farther upstream. *(Little Rock, AR)*

Los Angeles in Spanish means the angels. It's short for *Nuestra Señora de los Angeles de la Porciúncula*, or Our Lady of the Angels of the Little Portion. Now most people just say "L.A." *(Los Angeles, CA)*

Memphis is an African name. It is a city in Egypt. *(Memphis, TN)*

Miami could be Ottawan for mother. But it might come from Delaware, *we-mi-a-mik*, and mean all friends. Or it might be Ojibway. We don't know for sure. *(Miami, FL)*

Milwaukee is Algonquian, and means good land. *(Milwaukee, WI)*

Minneapolis is Sioux and Greek. Minnehaha means water falls. Polis means city. In Minneapolis there is a Minnehaha Falls, which means water falls waterfalls. *(Minneapolis, MN)*

New York is English, and is named for the Duke of York. Charles the Second gave him the colonies to look after. Before this, New York was Niew Amsterdam, which is Dutch. "Niew Amsterdam, Niew Amsterdam" is a little harder to sing. *(New York, NY)*

Phoenix is a Greek mythological bird that was born again from its own ashes. You may be familiar with Professor Dumbledore's phoenix. *(Phoenix, AZ)*

Pittsburgh is part English for William Pitt, a statesman. Burgh is the Scottish spelling of the French *bourg*, which means fort. Penn is for William Penn, but is also Welsh for headland. Sylvania comes from the Latin word for forest. *(Pittsburgh, PA)*

Portland is named for a Portland in England. *(Portland, ME)*

Portland is named for Portland, Maine. However, it could just as easily have been named Boston. A coin toss decided it. *(Portland, OR)*

St. Louis is named for the French King Louis IX, who was made a saint because he established laws, founded universities, and cared for the poor. *(St. Louis, MO)*

Salem comes from shalom, the Hebrew word for peace. *(Salem, MA)*

San Francisco is the Spanish name for St. Francis of Assisi, an Italian monk and religious reformer. *(San Francisco, CA)*

Santa Fe is Spanish for Holy Faith. *(Santa Fe, NM)*

Schenectady is Iroquian, probably for beyond the pines. *(Schenectady, NY)*

Seattle is named for a Salish Native American leader. *(Seattle, WA)*

Tombstone is English, and means grave marker. At first this city was probably hard to live in. *(Tombstone, AZ)*

Tuscaloosa is Choctaw, and means warrior-black. It probably refers to a real chief, Tascaluça. Groucho Marx once made a pun about this city and elephants with wiggly teeth. *(Tuscaloosa, AL)*

Waikiki is Hawaiian. It is a district of Honolulu. *(Waikiki, HI)*

Washington honors George Washington, the first president of the United States of America. *(Washington, DC)*

New York is English.

Chattanooga is Creek.

El Paso is Spanish.

Minneapolis, Minnesota, is part Sioux, part Greek.

New York is boastful, named for a nobleman.

Minneapolis doesn't care.
After all, her name is like a song.

El Paso is adventuresome,
means here's the river crossing.

But **Chattanooga** is steadfast.
Chattanooga is lofty.
Charming **Chat-ta-noo-ga** means
rocks rising to a point.

New York is English,
drinks tea from a china cup.
The nobleman he's named for
was, after all, a duke.
The Duke of York he was,
became James the Second,
the King of all England.
Imagine! A king!

Minneapolis, part Sioux.
Minneapolis, part Greek.
Greek polis means city.
Now, Minnea comes from Minnehaha,
means water falling, not
water laughing, ha ha.
Still, Longfellow (wonderful writer) liked this,
made Minnehaha Laughing Water,
heroine of the Song of Hiawatha.
Never mind.
City of the waterfall by the
water of the blue skies is
beautiful **Minneapolis**.
Minneapolis, Minnesota.

New York is English.
Thought, "How about a party?
I'll mail invitations.
I need some new friends.

Now, who, besides **Chattanooga,
Minneapolis,** and **El Paso**—
who, besides those three,
might like to attend?"

New York, who is English, invited
San Francisco, who is Spanish,

Chicago, who is Algonquin, and

Pittsburgh, Pennsylvania, who is equal parts English, Scottish, Latin, and Welsh.

New York was worried.
"Will this be a fiasco?
San Francisco is sensitive,
named for St. Francis
(Italian and holy),
who spoke with the birds.
And **Chicago** is fearsome,
ferocious. Has to be.
With a name like stinking onions,
you've got to stick up for yourself."

Then **New York** remembered
Minneapolis, Minnesota.

Minneapolis, Minnesota,
would unknot any scramble.

On the evening of the party,
his house looking really, very fine,
New York, nevertheless nervous,
checked his list
one last time.

Charlotte, who is German,
the first to arrive,
entered like a queen.
She's named for Charlotte Sophia,
Princess of Mecklenburg-Strelitz,
consort of George the Third,
so you shouldn't be surprised.

Now others arrived.
New York, who is English,
bowed everyone in.

"**Cheyenne,** I'm charmed.

Ah, **Ashtabula** . . .

Schenectady!"

Little Rock.

Biloxi.

Milwaukee, good to meet you.

Welcome, **Waikiki**.

The first minutes were quiet.

Dutch **Brooklyn** stood with
French **Des Moines:**

"Broken land" next to "of the monks."
Well, you can imagine.

St. Louis got a little pushy
(he is named for a crusader).

Buffalo felt out of place.
Was he named for a bison?
That doesn't make sense.
Could it be he is mongrel French?
Beau fleuve is so much nicer.

But then **Philadelphia** met **Memphis**,
and the good feelings started flowing.

Memphis is Egyptian.
      Philadelphia is Greek.
One is an ancient city in Africa.
      The other means brotherly love.

Beulah met **Bethesda**.
They're both Aramaic!

Amarillo mixed with
Baton Rouge, who mingled
with **Green Bay**.
That is yellow, red, and green.

Seattle greeted **Washington,**
who hello-ed **Tuscaloosa**—
they're all named for military men.

Well, the party,
an enormous success.

Los Angeles was angelic.
Santa Fe was faithful.
Phoenix rose from the ashes
at a quarter after ten.

Miami was motherly.
Atlanta chugged along.
Portland, Maine, hugged **Portland,** OR.
Anchorage was calm.

A thousand names,
a hundred languages,
a million, and a million, and a million people
name one nation.

Soon—too soon—
the last guests left
after their last cups of cocoa.
New York, who is English,
bowed everyone out.

"*Buenos noches,* **Las Vegas**.
Au revoir, **Lafayette**.
Darling **Salem,** shalom.
Tombstone! Good night."

New York put his feet up
and smiled at the evening.

El Paso was happy with a nice cup of tea.

Minneapolis, Minnesota,
read a little poetry.

Chattanooga gets up early.
Chattanooga has work to do.
Charming **Chattanooga** went straight to bed.

New York is English.

Chattanooga is Creek.

El Paso is Spanish.

Minneapolis, Minnesota, is part Sioux, part Greek.

Seattle

Anchorage

Portland

Minneapolis

Des Moines

Cheyenne

San Francisco

Las Vegas

Santa Fe

Amarillo

Los Angeles

Phoenix

Waikiki

Tombstone

El Paso